Noodles' & Albie's Mermaid Parade

Eric Bennett

Illustrated by Paige Monte

NOODLES AND ALBIE were at the edge of the ice, introducing Noodles' baby sister, Paige, to the sea. Not far away were world-famous penguin experts Jon and Ken, who were finishing up a frigid month of research on the Antarctic ice.

"I can't believe we finally set sail for home tomorrow," said Jon.

"Do you think we'll make it back to Brooklyn in time for the Mermaid Parade?" asked Ken.

"We're supposed to," said Jon. "I haven't missed a parade or the opening of the amusement park in years."

Upon hearing this, Noodles waddled over.

"Excuse me, sir," he said. "What's this about an amusement park?"

"Did you say something, penguin?" asked Jon.

"My name is Noodles, and this is my friend Albie, and, yes, I did. We love amusement parks."

"And parades!" added Albie.

"Well, Noodles and Albie, there's a place called Coney Island," said Jon. "It's the world's greatest amusement park."

"Every year, in June, they have a Mermaid Parade to officially open the park," said Ken.

"Mermaid Parade? What's that?" asked Albie.

"It's a parade where everyone has to dress in aquatic costumes," said Jon.

"Excuse me, but what's aquatic?" asked Paige.

"It means anything to do with water," said Ken.

"Like a fish?" asked Albie.

"Or a penguin?" added Noodles with a smile.

"Exactly!" said Jon.

"Well, I'd like to go!" said Noodles.

"Me, too!" said Albie.

"Okay," said Jon. "I'll ask the Captain, and you two ask your parents. If everyone says it's okay, we'll meet right back here tomorrow, same time."

The next morning, Captain Sonja welcomed them all aboard and off they went.

"Noodles, have you ever seen any other types of penguins?" Jon asked.

"You mean, like my friend Waddles?" asked Noodles.

"No," said Jon. "Not other penguins. Other types of penguins."

"I don't think so," said Noodles.

"In fact, there are 18 different types of penguins in the world," said Jon.

"Wow," said Noodles. "I never knew that."

"Well, you might be a penguin, but I'm the penguin expert," said Jon, laughing.

"Our first stop tomorrow morning is the Falkland Islands, where some of those other penguins live," Jon continued. I have to check on some instruments. Would you like to come along, Noodles?"

"Would I ever!" said Noodles.

The next morning, upon landing at the Falklands, Noodles and Jon set off. The first penguins Noodles encountered were King Penguins.

"Hey, what kind of penguin are you?" a King asked, staring up at Noodles.

"My name is Noodles, and I'm an Emperor penguin."

"Emperor Penguin? Big deal. My name's Henry, and I'm a King! And everyone knows Kings are the most important penguin!" proclaimed Henry.

"Oh, I don't think that's true," said Noodles. "I'm pretty sure Emperors are just as important as Kings."

"Seriously?" said Henry. "I run things around here, and nothing beats King Henry!"

"Hey, hey, hey! You're both great penguins," said Jon. "Noodles, you can be the Emperor of Antarctica, and Henry, you are obviously King of The Falklands. Now, Noodles, we have to get going if we're going to make that Mermaid Parade," Jon said with a wink.

"We're about to meet some Rockhopper penguins. But, be warned, they can be a little feisty, especially Rocko," said Jon.

"What do you mean by feisty?" said Noodles. "And who's Rocko?"

"Who are you looking at, shorty?" came a voice from the rocks above. Noodles looked up, and on the cliff ledges were the strangest little penguins he had ever seen.

"What do you mean by 'shorty'? Noodles asked. "You're not taller than me. You're just standing on some rocks."

"Ha," said Rocko. "Short and bald.""Yeah, where are your head feathers, baldy? Is that why you're wearing a hat?" said the first Rockhopper. "I'm an Emperor penguin, and I'm not bald. I just don't have feathers like you," explained Noodles.

Jon stepped between them. "Noodles, I'm all done. I think we should go."

"Now I know what feisty means," said an exasperated Noodles.

When Jon and Noodles reached the ship, they were surprised to find Henry and Rocko waiting for them.

"Henry heard that you guys are going to a Mermaid Parade," said Rocko.

"Sounds like a blast," added Henry.

"Well, compared to sitting on rocks all day, anything would be a blast," said Rocko.

"Can we PLEASE come along?" asked Henry and Rocko.

"Okay by me," said Jon.

"Sure... I guess," added Noodles with a shrug.

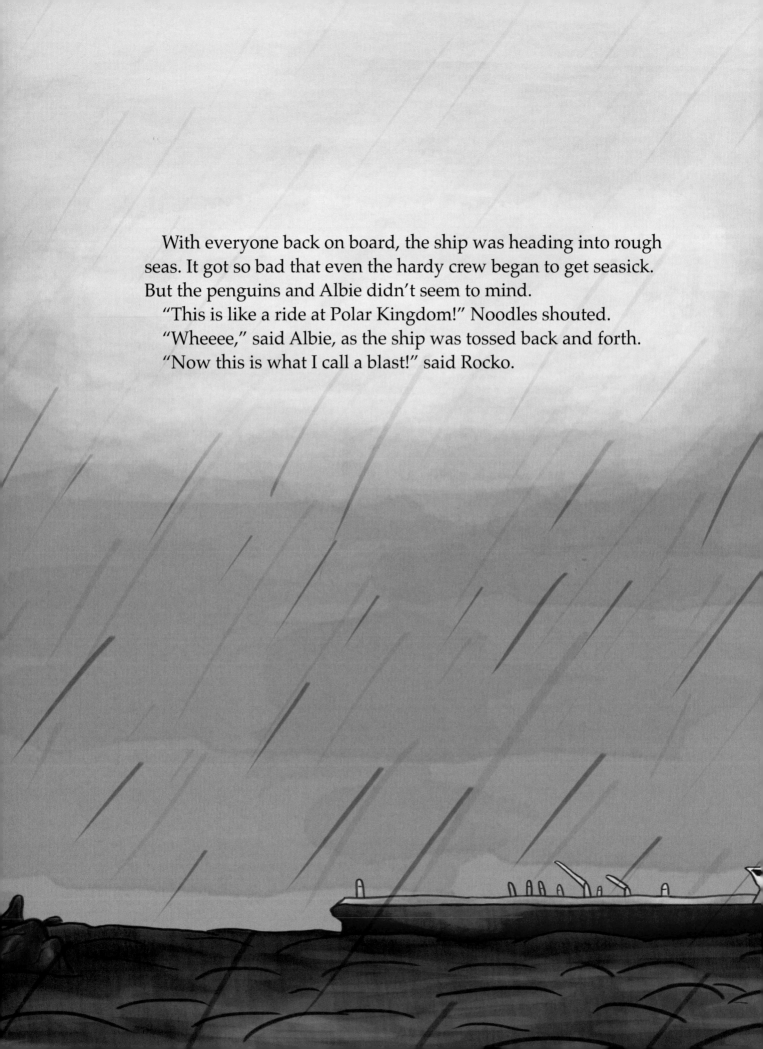

With everyone back on board, the ship was heading into rough seas. It got so bad that even the hardy crew began to get seasick. But the penguins and Albie didn't seem to mind.

"This is like a ride at Polar Kingdom!" Noodles shouted.

"Wheeee," said Albie, as the ship was tossed back and forth.

"Now this is what I call a blast!" said Rocko.

As nighttime fell, the storm grew worse, and in the distance the captain spotted an oil tanker heading for some rocks.

"I've contacted the tanker about those rocks, but I'm not sure if they can see them," said the Captain. "If they hit those rocks, it'll rip a hole in that ship, and its oil will spill out," said Jon. "That'll pollute the ocean for miles," said Ken. "It may take years to clean up!" "If only there were some lights to guide it around the rocks," said the Captain.

"Hey, I have an idea," said Noodles. "Why don't you attach some lights to us?"

"We can swim in this storm, no problem," said Henry.

"Just tell the tanker to follow us," said Albie.

"That's a great idea. I think I have just the thing!" said the Captain. "But we have to hurry."

"I'll contact the tanker and tell them to follow the lights."

"That was fun!" said Albie.

"It sure was," agreed Noodles. "I'm glad we got to help that ship."

"And wear those cool hats," added Rocko.

"Excuse me, Captain. Where we come from it's dark for many months at a time. Do you think we can keep these hats?" asked Noodles.

"They really would come in handy," said Henry.

"Oh, I think we can spare a few headlamps for our heroes," replied the Captain.

"Hey, that's one big green lady," said Noodles.

"And what are those?" asked Albie, pointing at the skyline.

"Buildings. That's where people work and live," said Jon. "Welcome to New York City."

"Wow!" said the four wide-eyed visitors.

"Here are your costumes," said Jon.

"We're going straight to Coney Island. I called my friend Lucy and she's already there, getting our parade float ready."

"Hey, guys," whispered Albie. "I think we won because the judges thought we were wearing costumes, but we really are just a fish and some penguins."

"I'm so happy," said a smiling Jon. "I've never been King of the Mermaid Parade before."

"Well, Jon, you might be King for a day," said Rocko, "but Noodles will always be the Emperor."

MERMAID PARADE
BEST COSTUME CONTEST

FIRST PLACE

ABOUT THE AUTHOR

Eric Bennett was raised in New York City. After graduating Queens College, he opened the world's first all-penguin shop at South St. Seaport. In time, Bennett began to offer his retail rookery online at penguingiftshop.com. Eric currently lives in Northampton, Massachusetts, with his two fun daughters and a few hundred penguins. This is his third book.

ABOUT THE ILLUSTRATOR

Paige Monte grew up near the Hudson River in New York. She obtained her BFA in Animation from Massachusetts College of Art and Design. Paige loves making art and telling stories about mermaids and sea life. She is very excited to have worked on this wonderful story for her first ever book. You can see more of Paige's work at paigemonteart.com.

Penguin Place Books
26 Main St. Northampton, MA 01060
413-584-5432
penguin@bway.net